WHAT THE MOON SEES

NANCY TAFURI

GREENWILLOW BOOKS · NEW YORK

The moon sees

bright stars.

The moon sees

quiet barnyards.

The moon sees

hooting owls.

The moon sees

empty streets.

The moon sees

silent playgrounds.

The moon sees

sleeping children.

And the moon watches

until the sun comes up.

NOW TURN THE BOOK AROUND

NOW TURN THE BOOK AROUND

until the moon comes up.

And the sun watches

busy children.

The sun sees

The sun sees

bustling streets.

The sun sees

sleeping owls.

The sun sees

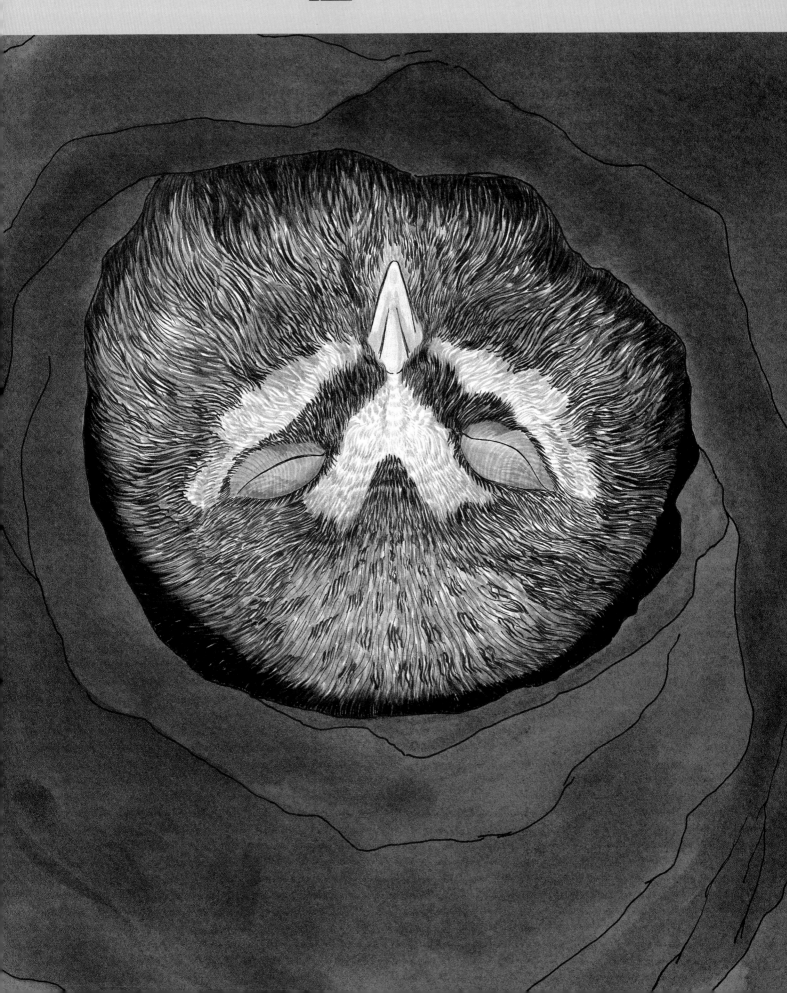

crowded barnyards.

blue skies,

The sun sees

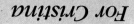

Library of Congress
Cataloging-in-Publication Data
Tafuri, Nancy.
What the sun sees,
what the moon sees /
by Nancy Tafuri.
p. cm.
Summary: Contrasts the world as viewed in sunlight and then the quiet night world in moonlight.
ISBN 0-688-14493-4 (trade)
ISBN 0-688-14494-2 (lib. bdg.)
[1. Day—Fiction. 2. Night—Fiction. 3. Sun—Fiction. 4. Moon—Fiction.] I. Title. PZ7.T117Wg 1997
[E]—dc20 96-20976 CIP AC